This book belongs to:

....

Note to parents and carers

Read it yourself is a series of classic, traditional tales, written in a simple way to give children a confident and successful start to reading.

Each book is carefully structured to include many high-frequency words that are vital for first reading. The sentences on each page are supported closely by pictures to help with reading, and to offer lively details to talk about.

The books are graded into four levels that progressively introduce wider vocabulary and longer stories as a reader's ability grows.

Ideas for use

- Although your child will now be progressing towards silent, independent reading, let her know that your help and encouragement is always available.

- Developing readers can be concentrating so hard on the words that they sometimes don't fully grasp the meaning of what they're reading. Answering the puzzle questions on pages 46 and 47 will help with understanding.

For more information and advice, visit www.ladybird.com/readityourself

Level 4 is ideal for children who are ready to read longer stories with a wider vocabulary and are eager to start reading independently.

Special features:

Full, exciting story

As soon as Snow White bit the apple, she fell and died.

When the dwarfs came back, they tried to help her, but it was too late. Snow White could not be woken.

The dwarfs were very sad.

39

38

Clear type

Richer, more varied vocabulary

Snow White grew up, and she looked more beautiful every day.

One day, when the queen went to her mirror it said, "Snow White is the fairest of them all."

Longer sentences

Detailed illustrations to capture the imagination

10

11

Educational Consultant: Geraldine Taylor

A catalogue record for this book is available from the British Library

Published by Ladybird Books Ltd
80 Strand, London, WC2R 0RL
A Penguin Company

001 - 10 9 8 7 6 5 4 3 2 1
© LADYBIRD BOOKS LTD MMXI
Ladybird, Read It Yourself and the Ladybird Logo are registered or
unregistered trade marks of Ladybird Books Limited.

ISBN: 978-1-40930-368-8
Printed in China

Snow White
and the Seven Dwarfs

Illustrated by Tanya Maiboroda

Once upon a time, a beautiful queen had a baby girl.

The baby's skin was as white as snow, and she had beautiful black hair. The queen called her baby Snow White.

But soon, the queen died and the king married again. The new queen was beautiful, but she was very wicked. She had a magic mirror. Every day she asked it, "Mirror, mirror, on the wall, who is the fairest of them all?"

And every day the mirror said, "You, Queen, are the fairest of them all."

8

Snow White grew up, and she looked more beautiful every day.

One day, when the queen went to her mirror it said, "Snow White is the fairest of them all."

The queen was angry. She didn't want to live with anyone more beautiful than herself.

She called for her huntsman and said, "Take Snow White into the forest and kill her."

So the huntsman took Snow White into the forest. They went on and on all day, but he could not kill her. She was too beautiful.

"Run away," he said. "The queen wants to kill you. You must never come back. If you do, you will die."

14

Snow White ran away into the forest. Soon, she came to a little house. She couldn't run any more, so she opened the door and went in.

In the house, she saw a table with seven little chairs. Then she saw seven little beds.

"These beds are so little," said Snow White. "Whoever could sleep in them?"

Snow White was so tired that she went to sleep on the beds.

Soon, the little men who lived in the house came back. They were seven dwarfs who worked in the mines. They saw Snow White sleeping.

"What is this beautiful girl doing in our house?" they asked.

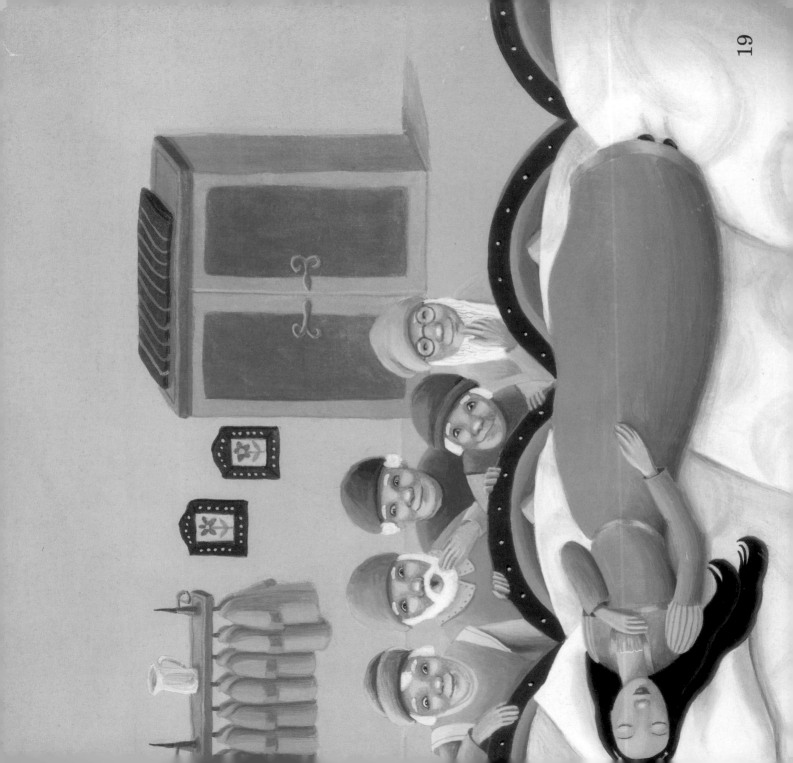

Suddenly, Snow White woke up.

"Who are you?" said Snow White.

"We are the seven dwarfs," said the biggest of the dwarfs.

Snow White told them that the wicked queen wanted to kill her, and that she had run away.

The dwarfs looked at one another. Then the biggest of the dwarfs said, "You must stay here. You will be safe in this house."

The dwarfs told Snow White that she must never talk to anyone who came to the door.

Back at the castle, the queen
went to her mirror.

"Mirror, mirror, on the wall,
who is the fairest of them all?"
she asked.

And the mirror said, "Snow White
is the fairest of them all."

The queen was very angry.
She put on some old clothes,
and went into the forest. There
she found the little house.

The dwarfs were out at work, so the queen knocked on the door.

"Do you want to see my beautiful ribbons?" she asked.

Snow White opened the door to look at the ribbons.

At once, the queen put a ribbon round Snow White's neck, so that Snow White could not breathe.

When the dwarfs came back and found Snow White, they took the ribbon off and put her to bed.

Soon, she woke up. They told her that she must never open the door to anyone, ever again.

But the next time the queen looked in the mirror, it said, "Snow White is the fairest of them all."

The queen was very angry again.

"I will kill Snow White once and for all," she said.

Once again, the queen put on old clothes and went to the little house. This time, she had some beautiful combs.

When she came to the house, she knocked on the door.

"The dwarfs told me not to talk to anyone who comes to the door," said Snow White.

"Then I will put a comb by the door and go," said the queen.

When the queen had gone, Snow White took the comb and put it in her hair. The comb had poison on it, and Snow White fell asleep.

When the dwarfs came back, they looked after Snow White and made her well again.

The queen didn't go to her magic mirror for some time.

But then one day, she asked the mirror, "Mirror, mirror, on the wall, who is the fairest of them all?"

And the mirror said, "Snow White is the fairest of them all."

The queen was angrier than ever. She went out to find Snow White one last time.

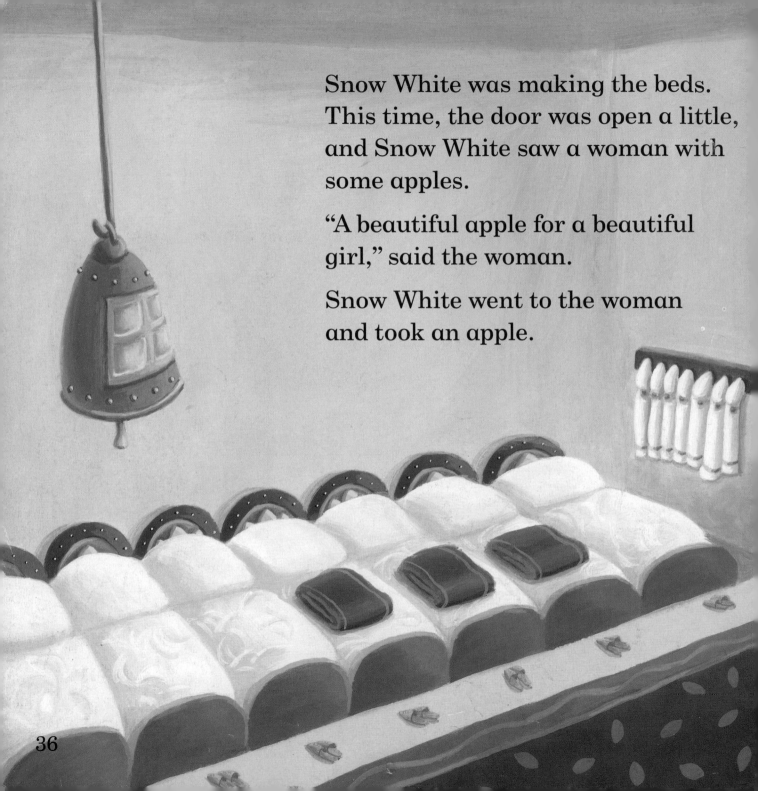

Snow White was making the beds. This time, the door was open a little, and Snow White saw a woman with some apples.

"A beautiful apple for a beautiful girl," said the woman.

Snow White went to the woman and took an apple.

As soon as Snow White bit the apple, she fell and died.

When the dwarfs came back, they tried to help her, but it was too late. Snow White could not be woken.

The dwarfs were very sad.

After a time, they put Snow White in a glass coffin on a hillside. She looked as if she was sleeping.

One day, a prince came by. He saw Snow White lying in the coffin, and fell in love with her.

The prince opened the glass coffin and kissed Snow White. The kiss woke her. She saw the prince, and fell in love at once.

"Will you marry me?" asked the prince.

"I will," said Snow White.

Very soon, Snow White and the prince were married and everyone came to see. The wicked queen was there, too. When she saw Snow White, she was so angry that she ran away and was never seen again.

And Snow White and the prince, and all the seven little dwarfs, lived happily ever after.

How much do you remember about the story of Snow White and the Seven Dwarfs? Answer these questions and find out!

- What magical thing did the queen own?

- Why was the queen angry?

- Who did the queen ask to kill Snow White?

- Whose little house did Snow White come to?

- Where did the seven dwarfs put Snow White when they thought she was dead?

- Who found Snow White lying in the glass coffin?

Look at these words. Unjumble them to make words from the story and then match them to the pictures.

swarfd

nows thiew

neueq

smunthan

cimag romirr

nicepr

Read it yourself
with Ladybird

The Three Billy Goats Gruff

Cinderella

Little Red Hen

Goldilocks and the Three Bears

The Enormous Turnip

The Magic Porridge Pot

The Ugly Duckling

The Emperor's New Clothes

The Gingerbread Man

Sleeping Beauty

Little Red Riding Hood

Town Mouse and Country Mouse

Sly Fox and Red Hen

The Three Little Pigs

Chicken Licken

Rumpelstiltskin

The Elves and the Shoemaker

Jack and the Beanstalk

Hansel and Gretel

Rapunzel

The Pied Piper of Hamelin

The Wizard of Oz

Heidi

Snow White and the Seven Dwarfs

Collect all the titles in the series.